Theft Of A Lifetime

LIANA BROOKS

OTHER WORKS

ALL I WANT FOR CHRISTMAS

All I Want For Christmas Is A Reaper
All I Want For Christmas Is A Werewolf

FLEET OF MALIK

Bodies In Motion
Change of Momentum

HEROES AND VILLAINS

Even Villains Fall In Love
Even Villains Go To The Movies
Even Villains Have Interns
Even Villains Play The Hero (books 1 – 3 omnibus)
The Polar Terror

TIME AND SHADOWS
The Day Before
Convergence Point
Decoherence

SHORTER WORKS

Fey Lights
If You Give A Skeleton A 3D Printer…
Prime Sensations
Darkness and Good

Find other works by the author at
www.lianabrooks.com

Theft Of A Lifetime

INKLET #64

LIANA BROOKS

Inkprint PRESS

www.inkprintpress.com

Print ISBN: 978-1-925825-66-4
eBook ISBN: 9798201668976

www.inkprintpress.com

National Library of Australia Cataloguing-in-Publication Data
Brooks, Liana 1983 –
Theft Of A Lifetime
68 p.
ISBN: 978-1-925825-66-4
Inkprint Press, Canberra, Australia
1. Fiction—Fantasy—Action & Adventure 2. Fiction—Crime 3. Fiction—Short Stories

First Print Edition: August 2021
Cover photo © Enrique Meseguer via Pixabay
Cover design © Inkprint Press
Interior art © Amy Laurens

THEFT OF A LIFETIME

"WE HAVE A PLAN," TRAE SAID, SMOOthing a weathered brown map across the cracked alehouse table.

A falling log cracked in the fireplace, sending off a shower of sparks and sputters. Somewhere behind the quiet bar the innkeep snored, and overhead the last of the beds had stopped their rhythmic squeaking. For now, they were alone with their plans.

Kinni turned the map to look at the rough terrain dividing them from their goal. "This isn't a plan."

"It will be." Trae took a charred stick and started drawing lines across the map. "We'll cross on the east under cover of darkness, slip past the outer defenses when they change guards during the first bell of night, and enter during the false dawn. This is victory!"

"Or death."

Trae shrugged.

"We've already lost too many," Kinni said. "This... is this worth it?"

His friend studied the map with the path over the rocky gorge and along the steep cliffs. "The Fordrakin Guard killed Shay and Jennell. If we don't do this..." Trae shook his head.

The best spellcaster and necromancer in the living lands were gone, bodies lost to unmarked graves. If the Fordrakin could do that...

Kinni crossed his arms, rubbing away a foreboding chill. "This is risky."

"Very," Trae agreed.

"When do we leave?"
"Now."

A sharp, brutally cold wind cut through Kinni's patched jacket as he clung to the smooth granite of the gorge. Moonlight flirted with him, coyly peeking out from behind streaming clouds to illuminate the next handhold, then darting away as he struggled to find a place to rest his foot.

Above him Trae kicked a rock loose, sending a tiny avalanche down to the dry riverbed below.

At least the night was cold enough that the patrols wouldn't wander far from the burning fires of the guard shacks. The road was several leagues away, well known and well protected.

Coming across the gorge was almost suicidally risky—and therefore unexpected.

Kinni's hand slipped and for a moment he dangled in the air, heavy boots pulling him down toward dark death.

"Come on." Trae grabbed his wrist and hauled him to the top. "We can't die here."

"We could," Kinni said. "Easily."

The wind battered at them in the moonlight, whipping them for daring to trespass on its wild domain.

"Dying here does not achieve our goal."

Kinni's fingers slipped to the enchanted dagger at his hip. Not his only weapon, of course. Not even his weapon of choice. But it was the one that mattered. The one he needed to use before the sun rose and hit its zenith, or all would be for naught.

Trae pulled at his arm. "Come on. The map says there's a good hiding spot ahead."

"A dead tree in a desert." It sounded as unlikely as survival.

"An ancient, twisted ironwood so tough no axe could fell it," Trae repeated the bard's story. "With gnarled roots thick as a strong man's arm that bite into the desert rock and hold back a cursèd darkness."

Kinni shook his head. "How many ales did you have last night? I swear I cut you off after two."

"Shush," Trae ordered, pushing him ahead to where a menacing shadow blocked out the lighter darkness of the night.

Shuffling forward, Kinni curled his lip in a sneer. "I'm just saying, when we're talking about seeking refuge in the darkest darkness, it's time to consider the possibility we might be in some ridiculous ballad. Those never end well for people like us."

"That's because people like us, in stories, don't know what we know. Remember, we have friends in grave places."

Almighty desert mother, Trae had definitely had more than two ales.

Kinni's foot slipped out from under him, sliding along the gritty sand into an unexpected opening.

Trae pushed him the rest of the way down. Under the ground. Out of reach of the skittish moonlight. Far from the safe and practical life he'd led in the great city of Onthizan.

His fingers played along the dagger's handle again, the cold gold curved by the smithy's skill into head of roaring lion. If he closed his eyes, he could picture the first night he'd held it; taste the woodsmoke and honey wine, touch the silky flowers of the wedding and the soft skin of his beloved.

The ground trembled under the feet of the Fordrakin Guard above.

Like a snake, Kinni watched in the darkness, waiting for his moment to strike.

The cave led them straight to the dark stone wall, just as the map had promised—despite Kinni's misgivings.

"Do you think they use magic to smooth the stone?" Trae asked from halfway up as he slipped again and fell closer to the ground.

"Has to be something." The rope around Kinni's waist tightened as he drove another piton between the massive stones. "Had to be magic to fit these stones so tight. I've met kingdom treasuries with more holes than this wall." All to his delight and personal enrichment. Though those days were long gone.

But there was always more than gold in the treasuries. Secrets were hidden there. Bones too, more than once. After awhile he'd found he couldn't look away any more. Couldn't feign ignorance while the rich pillaged the poor souls in their cities.

Trae was along for the same reasons. He'd been born wealthy enough. His future had been promising, but then the wrong person had asked Trae for the wrong thing. They'd underestimated his simmering anger, mistook it for acceptance…

And so here they were now, climbing the enchanted walls of a forbidden keep in search of a bauble that could save the world.

Terribly cliché, really. World-saving magic shouldn't ever be kept in something that could be tucked into a pocket. Kinni would have told anyone— had they bothered to ask—that enchanting a mountain was the way to go. Or ensorcelling a sea.

No one stole entire oceans.

Not yet, at any rate.

Although he could come up with a plan if he had a few days free and a suitable, pecuniary, incentive.

"It's starting to get light," Trae said, his hand finally casting a shadow against the dark gray walls. "A couple of minutes is all we've got."

Kinni looked up at the last bit of the climb. "We can't do this careful."

"Then do it well," Trae said as he pulled a steel arrow from his belt. Reaching up, he stabbed between the stones, using the arrow as a piton, resting his weight on it just long enough to swing up and stab another in.

It was a dangerous risk to take, but that was the only way to win dangerous games.

Brushing his hand across the cold of the lion's head dagger, Kinni followed Trae up the wall, abandoning rope and reason to make up for lost time.

They stopped near the top, fingers curled around the edge of the parapet as they watched the rising sun and shadows.

"You sure about this?" Kinni asked. "Once we're in..."

"I'm in," Trae said without hesitation. "This is it. This is the only way to get what we want."

"It won't be easy."

Trae flashed him the grin that had gotten them into trouble in every city between the Port of Tensheirs and the frozen streets of Yesling. "You know me, I like a challenge." And Trae was just the sort that would see fighting death as a challenge.

Was it worth it?

Kinni thought of the prize at the end. His heart raced, feeding a hunger inside him for his goal. Licking his lips in greedy anticipation, he smiled back at Trae. "Let's go."

How strange they must have looked to the distant and uncaring gods. Two thieves scrambling over the wall to the greatest stronghold. Two friends willingly charging into the place of darkest magic. All with smiles on their faces and a bitter wind teasing their hair.

The upper walk was silent. Whatever guards might have been on duty for the night were inside, warming themselves and ignoring the dawn creeping over the empty desert outside. There was no easy crossing and—unless some idiot tried to climb the gorge—no one was likely to come over that wall.

Kinni and Trae found the narrow stairs spiraling down to the courtyard.

"Ready?" Trae loosened the pouch at his belt. "This is the risky part."

Kinni glared at his friend and his gift for understatement.

"I'll give you a distraction," Trae continued, "but it won't take long—"

"It's a lock," Kinni said. "Me plus lock. What happens?"

"It's an *enchanted* lock," Trae said.

Kinni shrugged. "So were the ones on Vitilien Prison, but I got you out.

So were the locks on the treasury of Hazmin the Untouchable. Got the treasure out."

"And touched Hazmin, as I recall." Trae grinned.

The smile was infectious. Kinni grinned back. "Hazmin didn't call for the guards until after I was gone." He patted his friend's back. "Come on. The hours are burning away. We have to have this done by noon. And morning comes late in winter."

Already the sun was racing for the midpoint of the sky. The angry, black clouds gathering on the horizon would not change anything. There were certain rules that couldn't be broken, decrees of the gods and laws of magic that even a thief like himself couldn't find a way around.

This had to be done before noon or his prize would slip out of his grasp forever.

Trae clicked his tongue, stood up,

and crushed a curious blue pearl between his fingers.

It seemed for a moment like Trae was made of smoke. Kinni's eyes watered as they tried to focus, but his gaze kept sliding away to the ancient stonework. Finally, when he couldn't even force his head to turn in the sound of Trae's breathing, he nodded. "It's working."

"Count to ten." Trae laughed, his voice fading like a bad dream.

It wasn't an invisibility spell, not exactly. It just made people want to look elsewhere. To forget what they saw or what they heard.

It was a childish sort of spell, one any good security force would know how to handle.

But that was exactly why it was the distraction.

"Eight. Nine." Kinni took a deep breath. "Ten.

The courtyard exploded with sound.

Shattered rock scythed through the air.

An alarm went up, a great horn calling everyone to battle.

Kinni stood, pulled the jacket tighter across his chest as he buttoned the top button and pulled a red scarf across his mouth. The guard he'd borrowed it from had been well compensated with a free dinner, some light flirtation from the barmaid, and a good night's sleep courtesy of one of Trae's myriad of tiny vials.

Guards were rushing out of every door, with blood-stained cloaks and bloodshot eyes focused on the commotion. They near trampled each other as they fought for the right to defend their keep.

It was nothing to sashay through them, moving with the flow, ebbing back as they avoided a collision, moving forward once again as space opened between the ranks. Across the courtyard and to the golden door…

It was an overlay, naturally. Pure gold was too soft to make an adequate door. Although one rather stupendously stupid king across the desert in Platrilk had made doors of gold. By the time Kinni had gotten there, most the door was gone, along with all the easily movable gems. He'd taken several scrolls with the burial places of dead kings to console himself and then spent half a year living quite well off the pilfered grave goods.

Those had been happier days. Easier ones.

He ran finger across the lock to the Fordrakin treasury. It stung with a biting chill.

Kinni lifted his finger to his nose and inhaled. The smell of the desert wind and the Fordrakin guards was tinged with the scent of cloyingly sweet sand viper venom that had been left out in the sun too long.

A clever attempt, to be sure, but not even magic could keep viper venom toxic for long. Especially if the target had built up an immunity to it long ago. Not by choice, in Kinni's case, but he'd learned to work with the favors the gods granted him.

Behind him there was chaos.

In front of him there was a little jiggle of the torsion wrench and the rake.

Several pins in the lock turned and were stuck. Another jiggle. Another swipe of the rake. A wiggle. A tuck. A quick flick of the rake to catch a loose pin.

The door fell inward a few precious centimeters.

"Well done," Trae said, coming into focus beside him as the spell wore off.

"It was easy." There was no luck in saying it was too easy, but it had been. The lock had been designed to give any thief a false sense of security. The knowledge weighed on him like a dead man's shroud.

This was for Shay and Jennell.

This was for all they had already lost.

This was the theft of a lifetime.

Trae led the way, murmuring can-trips he'd learned in their travels to nullify the enchantments guarding what lay inside.

The only light came from high above, sunbeams filtered through the growing storm that gathered in the pockets of openings in the stone. Dust motes danced in the slender spotlights like a forgotten festival viewed from the stars.

Heart thumping, throat tight, Kinni turned the last corner to see the room where the glowing treasure waited.

Piles upon piles of enchanted moon pearls, each glowing brighter than the sun.

A radiant, captivating treasure.

Enough jewels for a thousand life-times.

Kinni's fingers closed around the lion-headed dagger.

Someone clapped.

Trae froze, hand above the treasure.

Cruel chuckles echoed around the room.

The shroud of fate tightened around Kinni as he slowly turned.

A man stood framed by the doorway and darkness. Ashen skin the color of bleached bones, pale cobweb hair, and sparkling, ocean-dark eyes. The master of the Fordrakin smiled piti-lessly at them.

"Murderer," Trae hissed.

The master sneered as he laughed. "Murder? Is that what you accuse me of, little thief? As if you've never taken something that wasn't your own to keep you alive."

Kinni tried to count the guards he saw in the shadows, but there were too many. They'd never be able to fight their way free. Not holding the treasure.

Probably not even if they abandoned their goal and quit the game now.

"You had no right to kill Shay!" Trae pulled the short sword from its sheath. "She never crossed your path, never cause you trouble. Your guards were not threatened by her."

"Do you think stealing a few baubles from me will change anything?" the master asked, his wine red robe shivering in a magical breeze. "Your intrusion is that of a gnat! You are nothing to me. A momentary annoyance."

The lion's head cut into Kinni's palm, the pain bringing him back to the moment. "Trae?"

"Yeah?" His friend stepped closer, sword at the ready.

"You ready?"

"Ready."

They charged as one, chasing the true prize. There weren't baubles and gems that could buy them what they wanted. Not anymore. But blood could pay the price.

Screaming, they cut into the guards of Fordrakin, the magical monsters who ruled the western desert with iron fists. This was the time for victory or death.

Pain seemed like a hollow memory.

Kinni groaned and rolled over on a bare floor. It was stone and not stone all at once. His body felt heavy and light. Around him was darkness and still perfect sight.

"So," Trae said, "this is death."

"Must be," Kinni agreed, standing without pain, or cold, or warmth. The lack of sensation was eerie. He could see the memory of the guard's jacket covering his body but he felt naked, and not in a fun way. "How much time has passed?"

Trae fumbled with his vest and finally pulled out what looked like a tiny star. It was something else, the vision of a spell or the memory of a hope or something completely other that Kinni couldn't define. It was beautiful and terrible all at once.

A dream and a nightmare.

Death seemed to be full of contradictions.

"Little over an hour left," Trae said. "We should hurry."

"A few more minutes alone with the gems would have helped," Kinni said as he pulled out the lion's head dagger. "I knew we were rushing things."

"Some things have to be rushed," Trae said. "Get to work."

The dagger was the only thing that felt real. It still held weight, and the eternal chill of unforgiving gold. Kneeling, Kinni dragged the enchanted dagger across the unstone of the unreal floor, carving in sigils. Speaking true names into the lifeless realm.

The air around him filled with whispers. If he closed his eyes, he could almost feel the breath of the speakers on his face. Almost feel their cold hands pulling at him, tugging at his clothes, demanding his attention.

He ignored them, turning in a circle and repeating the carvings a second time. A third. A fourth. A fifth. A sixth.

The room was growing warmer, more real.

He could feel the grit of dirt under his hands, the pressure of his body pushing his knees into the ground.

Light was forcing the darkness back.

Not a celestial light like the filtered sunstreams or trapped moonbeams, but the light of a living fire. Hot, red, pulsing light that had a heartbeat and a memory of music.

He carved the sigils a seventh time and then lifted the dagger, kissing the little lion's head. "Come on," he whispered. It wasn't part of the ritual or any prayer that would reach the gods; this was for him. "Come on, Jennell. Listen to me. Look for me."

A low hum filled the room, like the rumble of a distant drum echoing off a mountain pass. Heat built around him, tongues of unseen flame licking his skin as icy cold hands grabbed at him.

The sigils all around him burst into fire. A raging, vicious bonfire that caged him but did not touch him.

Kinni pushed a flame away like he would an errant puppy and stepped out of the ring. "Time?"

"A quarter hour left," Trae said, arms folded as he watched the fire.

Kinni grimaced. "I didn't think it would take that long."

"It takes as much time as it takes."

"Still, if we—" Kinni stopped talking as a woman walked into the room.

She was beautiful. More beautiful than any treasure or vista. More beautiful than any fabled queen or untouchable princess. Her hair was brown as a muddy farm field and her suntanned skin had pale white scars from a lifetime of survival. Her eyes were also brown, stunning, like sunlight on polished bronze. It didn't matter that she wore a ripped, woolen dress of faded green or that she had no gems. She was the only treasure his heart desired.

Kinni held out a hand. "Jenelle?"

"Kinni!" She rushed toward him, wrapping her warm arms around his neck, clinging to him. "What are you doing here? I told you to live." Her hands framed his face. "I told you to save yourself."

"I did." He'd run from the clearing. Let the soldiers haul her body away.

Let them leave his love to the vultures. "But I didn't promise to stay away forever. We had a few weeks, according to the priestess, until your soul was weighed."

Jenelle raised her eyebrows in amused disbelief. "So you thought, what, you'd steal me from death? Kinni, my darling, that's impossible."

"Not quite," Trae said.

Kinni looked over at his friend who had his arm wrapped around the waist of the lovely Shay. Her long white hair still had obsidian beads tied to her braids, although the ceremonial, silver gray robe she wore hadn't been what she died in in.

He nodded to her. "Hello, Shay."

"Hello, thief." She smiled kindly. "I see you've gotten in trouble without us around."

"I'd like to get in an entirely different type of trouble," Kinni said, hugging Jenelle tighter. "But it's going to take the theft of a lifetime. And, for that, I need the best spellcaster to ever live, and the world's greatest necromancer. One so powerful she can turn desert to living farmlands and dry rivers into rushing water."

Shay raised an eyebrow. "You'll be legendary."

"No, we're stealing the legend," Trae said. "We died in the treasury of Fordrakin Keep. Our blood seeped into the bones of the walls made from souls."

Slow realization stole over Jenelle's face. His lover looked up at him, joy radiating from her smile. "Really?"

Kinni nodded with an eager smile.

"And you brought my dagger?"

He held out the lion-headed dagger of death for her to take.

Jenelle's cackle echoed in death's realm. "Oh, that bitter, soul-sucking liche won't know what hit him."

"We have to hurry though," Trae

said. "Your time between life and death is almost over. If we don't go now, we won't go back to our lives, we'll go to... whatever's next."

With a flourish, Jenelle twirled the dagger in her hand. "Shay, babes, you know what I need."

Kinni stepped back to watch the love of his life—and death—work.

Her hands twisted as Shay filled the room with magic and stars. A million memories poured into the space between them.

The spicy scent of markets and the lonely sent of nights alone on the rooftop bed. The sound of crashing waves, clashing swords, calling rocs. The color of dresses and disguises and tapestries.

All of it twisted around Jenelle, flowing and tangling and braiding itself until the memories became— almost—something he could touch. But he had no magic for that. Only a necromancer could reach into the depths and find the life-ending pain that fed the Fordrakin Guard, that kept their master alive—and that could be reversed.

The twisting memories became a snake, a fanged desert viper.

Jenelle raised the lion-headed dagger high and stabbed down, killing the snake, reversing the flow of memory, stealing life from death.

Rushing forward, Kinni caught Jenelle as she fell, easing her to the ground and shielding her as the realm of death shattered around them.

Necromancers were meant to bring people back from the dead, not walk into the land of the dead and break out.

But that's what he wanted.

The theft of a lifetime.

The theft of her lifetime, stolen back from the gods of death, snatched from the wizard who would use her hours to prolong his own life, given back to his beloved so they could be together again.

Far overhead the midday sun broke through the heavy clouds to shine on the fallen Keep, and a flower, long ago trampled by thoughtless travelers, unfurled pale purple petals as it lived once again.

Jenelle rolled away, stretching and laughing as the sun shone down on her face.

Kinni sat beside her smiling.

"You two," Shay said with a forgiving sigh.

"We're the best thieves ever," Trae said. "Ever."

Kinni pulled Jenelle to him for a kiss. "And, for victory or death, we always have a plan."

THE MAKING OF *THEFT OF A LIFETIME*

Back in 2019 a friend sent me a call for an anthology asking for *"Ocean's 11* with ogres and trolls. *The Italian Job* pulled off using hippogriffs. *Good Fellas* done with dark fae. *Leverage* by way of Gandalf and Merlin."

And so I sat down to try and come up with something.

"We have a plan."

...The characters did, but I didn't. I wasn't sure what was happening, what was being stolen, or what the ending was. I just knew the characters wanted to steal something and death wasn't a problem.

From there I winged it. I tossed in fantasy world tropes: thieves, swords, and curses. Added in the usual bag of tricks: rogues, lockpicks, and guile. Mixed it together with a sharp smile and a wink, and this is what I had.

Something promising but strange.

A moment in another world where everything matters—and nothing.

Read more by Liana Brooks!

CHANGE OF MOMENTUM: CHAPTER ONE

THE HYPERTRAM FROM RYUN to Kytan was running three minutes late, a silver-blue moonbeam racing across the golden desert. It was one of the little inefficiencies that made Malcolm Long hate ground travel. That and the other passengers, of course.

Waving off an offer of food from the refreshment cart, he settled into a seat on the port side of the tram and bullishly stared out the window as they rushed across the barren rock between the city-states.

High overhead, a shining Koenig-1-11 caught the sunlight as it turned for a landing in Dreyun to the north.

Long's lips twitched into a frown as he pulled out his ever-present palm pad to take notes. The one-elevens were supposed to be phased out by now. Blue Sky Air Transport had been sold off six weeks ago to Lethe, and Lethe was replacing the one-elevens with the Koenig-360, a plane with a fabulous interior and fuel consumption that made him wince.

He assumed that was why Lethe had contacted his offices two days ago to request this meeting. They were paying for his travel, and had offered a consulting fee that was generous without being obscene.

The whole set-up made the hair on the back of his neck stand up.

Senior engineers at small research firms did not generally get attention like this. Especially since he hadn't published anything in over a year. His team had been busy, and he'd been juggling too many projects to finish anything of substance.

If this was about the Koenig-360s, he could handle the matter in a couple of weeks. If it wasn't…

An old fear clawed up his throat.

For a moment the crowded tram was silent, devoid of oxygen, cold as the dark between stars. Memories of pain and rage threatened to destroy him. His heart raced as he fought the fear. Pulled it under.

Drowned it in the memories of today.

That had been another life.

Another name.

A time of power and cruelty—because the two always went hand in hand. But it was the past. He'd left the islands and there was no way Lethe could know who he had been.

Lips twitching into a grim smile, he checked his watch as the rocks gave way to the cultivated terraces of Kytan. Red rock formations ringed what were laughably called terraformed plateaus, bordered first with grain crops dividing the desert from the cultivated countryside, and then the land rippled inward past pools of pale pink water lilies, and into a sea of blue-green iridescent irises that sparkled like a dragonfly's wing.

Kytan was famous for the blooms that appeared for six weeks during the height of the Descent wedding season. Right now, the city-state was over-flowing with tourists who wanted to wander the parks and young couples taking engagement photos for next summer.

The tram went straight to the hanging gardens hiding the terraced buildings at the heart of the city. The air was cooler there under the shade of the vines, effervescent with the scent of falling water, and the crowd hurried past him to catch the city transports while he walked, briefcase in hand, along a stream-lined road.

The artisinal waterway was filled with silvery-blue fish that swam through the sun-dappled water against the current flowing down from the step pyramids at the city center.

The original home of the Imperial Governor of Malik IV, designed to match the legendary summer palace of Emperor Insei Qui the Third, the pyramids in the center of the city were an architectural wonder, covered in towering waterfalls and fronds and vines of greenery. Great stone mountains built in the desert plain and covered with a deep green jungle, with flowers of brilliant white and pink burning along the branches like captured stars. The whole city sparkled like the dead emperor's scepter, exactly as the first arrivals from the old Empire had hoped.

"A thousand years of freedom and still we bow," Long murmured to himself. He couldn't remember the rest of the poem now, but he remembered when he'd first heard it, in the halls at school spoken by a girl who'd both captivated and challenged him.

She would have appreciated the architecture of Kytan.

Probably had the opportunity to, considering her family and wealth.

Or perhaps not.

With the powerful families on the first continent, it all depended on who you knew and who you were allied with.

The Longs were a small family with no allies, unless his mother's book club friends counted, which he personally didn't feel they needed to. A family name, the right genes, a pittance of an inheritance, and an acre of land somewhere out in the wilds between city-states. It had been enough to get his family off the islands along the edge of the second continent and earn him a scholarship to the most prestigious university, but it wouldn't keep him alive if the Lethes wanted him dead. Especially not here in their capital city.

"I suppose I should have asked for a bodyguard," he muttered to himself. One of the lab interns had the height and reach to be a good shield—but also the personality of a frightened rabbit, which might have made the graceless man more a liability than an asset.

Long followed the streams to the step pyramid and walked up the wide steps until he reached the main entrance.

The arched glass doors opened into a chilled atrium, where the light passing through the waterfalls outside rippled and splashed over the dark marble floor.

Jewel-colored hummingbirds zipped past, chasing each other to the background music of a drowsy orchestral melody.

He felt he should applaud the theatrics, but restrained himself instead to a small half-smile.

The Lethes didn't sound like the kind

of people who would enjoy his sense of humor.

A man in the Lethe colors of deep purple and slate gray approached him, white hair slicked back to an opalescent sheen. "May I help you, sir?"

"Doctor Malcolm Long. I have an appointment."

"Certainly, sir. If you'll please follow me."

He gestured to a bank of black lifts behind a discreet marble reception desk. The greeter stepped around and peered at a screen that Long had the good manners not to peek at.

Or at least not to get caught peeking at.

"You're a few minutes early, sir," the greeter said, glancing up at him with a moue of censure.

"My apologies. I have the day free if you would like me to wait." He must have rushed. And now I look too eager, he berated himself. On time was on time. Eager looked weak. Late was disrespectful. It was these little social mores that kept the culture of Descent afloat.

The greeter shook his head. "No, I apologize, sir. The computer recalculated the time based on the tram delay. You have arrived on schedule, but a few minutes later would have been acceptable as well. If you'll take lift number seven, sir, it will take you to your meeting room."

That wasn't much information to go on.

Today's invitation had come from Lethe Corp, but without a signature. It was one of the annoying habits of the business people on the first continent that they used to keep their rivals guessing. Not knowing who he was meeting with meant he couldn't study or prepare for the meeting, not unless he wanted to study the several hundred middle managers, division leads, and board members.

He stepped into the mirrored elevator and tried to avoid glancing at his reflection, afraid he'd catch himself glaring and remember what a bad idea it was to get caught up in the machinations of political fanatics.

The mirror image glared back anyway.

For good reason, too; he should have worn a touch of Lethe purple somewhere to show a willingness to work together. The dark gray suit with a white shirt was a little too neutral. Long jerked the edge of one cuff straighter, an expression of annoyance tugging at his lips. He suppressed that too. This was a stupid risk to take. But declining, he suspected, would have proven fatal.

The door to the lift opened to a long, wide room with a row of slit windows overlooking the city. The only furniture was a white stone desk, carved to look like it had grown out of the stone floor. The walls were lined with silent waterfalls that pooled around the edge of the room, filled with small green reeds that had either been genetically engineered for the poor lighting or were fake; he couldn't tell at this distance.

At the desk, a woman was silhouetted by the window light, her pale hair swept up into a coiling, sleek up-do and held in place by a pin with a dripping chain of amethysts that matched her silk shirt. She was framed by the jungle outside, a pale diamond in the city of jewels. The effect was stunning, albeit contrived.

Long waited in front of the lift for her to acknowledge him as a dark suspicion formed.

Several minutes crept by before the woman finished her work, turned off her screen and stood.

Recessed lights in the ceiling turned on as she moved, spotlighting Sonya Lethe, the sole heir of the Lethe fortune.

Fear crawled down his spine with cold fingers.

This is what a fish feels like when it sees a shark. I always wondered.

"Doctor Long, please, come in," she said from behind the desk. "I'm delighted you could make time in your schedule to come to Kytan today."

"The delight is mine," he said, repeating the proper polite phrasing. "I've been looking for an excuse to come to Kytan."

"Wedding season," Sonya said with a slink of a smile. "Is there someone you were hoping to show the flowers to?"

"Much to my mother's dismay, there is not."

Sonya walked around her desk and perched on the front edge. "Yes, she is Nettie Amherst of the Northland Amhersts, isn't she?"

"The last of that line to bear the Amherst name, yes." Sonya had done her homework, both a threat and a show of strength. Or maybe she thought it put them on equal footing. After all, any schoolchild raised on Descent could name the Lethe heirs back to the first ship.

"Perhaps your future spouse will see fit to revive the name. Long is...." She pursed her lips as she looked him up and down in an appraising way. "...Perhaps a little generic?"

He let the insult pass with a smile. "My father says it's a dialect word from the Grizhjan System meaning 'dragon'. I make it a rule never to argue translations with a linguist."

Sonya laughed. It was a calculated move, the arch of her neck, the degree of her smile, the uplift of her breasts, all mathematically designed to hide the fact that the muscles around her eyes never moved.

She wasn't amused, she was manipulating him.

There were few things in the world that felt worse.

Long waited her out. Social graces did not require him to laugh along with her, so he didn't.

"Doctor Long, you look so grim. I do not like grim faces at business."

"Forgive me, Miss Lethe, I wasn't sure what response you anticipated. My name is not often a topic of conversation."

She smiled with an apologetic head tilt. "Engineers. You're always so delightfully focused, aren't you?"

"It's been mentioned before."

"Excellent." Sonya nodded. "Focus, I believe, is something this project needs. Please, take a seat."

She brushed her hand along a control set in the stone desk and a chair materialized to one side, perfectly set to give the occupant a view of both the city and Sonya at their best angles.

Long regarded the chair with quiet suspicion. It was a trap, that much was obvious, but he wasn't sure exactly what kind.

Days like this, he thought about throwing it all away and moving back to the islands.

But then he'd never be able to fly again. And flying again was the only reason he kept breathing. Everything else was lost to him, but maybe, one day, he could reclaim the sky.

"It's quite safe," Sonya assured him as she took her own seat behind the desk. "The matter transporter is something new our research and development team is working on. It could replace all travel one day."

All the more reason to hate it.

Aloud he said, "I'd heard of research along those lines, but I thought we were decades away from a breakthrough." Unless someone was getting tech from the space fleet that had landed on the third continent. He, like most people, wasn't privy to the fine details of the treaty the planetary representative had signed with them, but he felt certain the tech they'd brought with them was off limits.

"This can only move objects a few feet. But it is fun to bring a chair in from the closet at the touch of a button. There's an awe factor I appreciate." She sat back with a smug smile, the empress on her throne.

"I can imagine." He took a seat and dutifully surveyed the view of the city.

Sonya sat in the chair across from him, blonde hair framed by the shimmering blue flowers. "Tell me, Doctor Long, do you have your father's gift for languages?"

The question blindsided him and he let a frown slip. "No. Some, I suppose. I speak all the regional cants of the first and second continents and can read the Journals Of Discovery in the original Imperial Script, but that's a talent any well-educated person on Descent can boast of." Especially since the dialects only changed a handful of slang terms between all of them. Calling them languages was a bit of an insult to the idea of diversity, really.

"You claim to have no gift for languages, but you broke the hardest cipher we know while at university." She laughed. "What a shame everyone isn't as lacking in gifts."

"Ah," he said, shrugging one shoulder in dismissal. "Cryptography is a ghost from my misguided youth." And he hadn't broken the cipher alone. The key to the whole thing had been in an obscure text his classmate had found.

Technically, he should have credited her, but that would have required finding her after the move to Descent, and he hadn't had the resources. And she was unlikely to want to speak to him ever again anyway.

"I work exclusively in aeronautical science now. That was why I thought you'd called me in, to solve the fuel efficiency problems with the Koenig-360?" He let the opening dangle.

Sonya waved the comment aside. "Planes are relics. We can burn all the fuel we want. In a few years the new matter transporters will be the foundation of Lethe's transportation division. Let the Koenigs fly. This project is much more time sensitive." She held up a datcube, black and small enough to be concealed in his fist.

Long raised an eyebrow in question.

"This belonged to one of my employees. At the time of his death he had no heir, so the data became company property."

How convenient for Lethe.

"My techs have been able to decrypt a portion of the data on here, but the rest is beyond them. We've applied to other experts Lethe already has a working relationship with, but neither were able to decrypt it. Both experts mentioned you." She held the datcube out to him.

It was heavier than its size suggested. Someone had coated it in the anti-theft paint that had been popular for the past two years—which meant it wasn't too old to be recoverable—but on one side he felt an indentation, as if someone had pierced the cover with a fingernail.

It was all too easy to picture the previous owner holding this in a death grip in their final moments.

A sense of inevitable dread settled over him. It had been a mistake accepting the Lethe's offer. A mistake to be found on their radar at all. If he couldn't untangle himself—quickly—he would undoubtedly meet the same fate as the datcube's luckless owner.

"Have you considered the possibility that the information is corrupted?" Long asked. "I can guess which experts you would speak to, and who would recommend me, and there's very little I could do that they wouldn't have. There's no point in wasting your time if the data isn't salvageable."

Sonya shrugged. "I give it a twelve percent chance of being corrupted. It might be a keyed cypher, but the balance of probability says it's most likely an encryption."

"And the data?"

"Time sensitive only because of the employee's death."

A thin thread of hope appeared. "I realize it's tactless to ask, but is this datcube part of an ongoing investigation into that death? My clearance for several of my projects requires me to steer clear of the Jhandarmi and all local constabulary."

Please say yes.

Sonya gave him another calculated smile, this one undoubtedly meant to make her look innocent and charming. "The employee died because of a burst heart. The coroner ruled it death of natural causes."

The coroners of Descent would rule a stab wound death by natural causes if the right people asked. It was a line of thought he didn't dare to follow. "The best I can offer is to look at the encryption. Without seeing it I can't tell you anything more."

"Can you have a status report to me by the end of the week?" Sonya asked with a polite smile that said 'No' wasn't an acceptable answer.

Three days to unlock the datcube and analyze the contents was a tight timeline if he wanted to focus on his other work, but it was doable. He nodded. "A status report, but nothing more. Do you have a copy of the cube that I can take with me?"

Her lips slipped into an uncharacteristic grimace. "That is our only copy."

"Ah." He set it down on the desk between them. "That makes security problematic."

"Your lab is secure?" she asked.

"The research lab is, but the outer office is designed with client comfort in mind."

Sonya nodded in understanding. "The datcube will be sent by armed courier. Lethe can offer you the standard security fee for priority technology as well as a consultant fee." She twisted the screen on her desk he could see the numbers.

Standard fees, nothing that raised any red flags, although the whole affair seemed suspect.

"If you are able to decode the data, there will be a sizable bonus. Have you ever worked with Lethe before?"

"I've never had the pleasure." Just as he'd never had the pleasure of being burned alive before. It was one of those little life-threatening things he'd made sure to avoid.

She pulled a paper contract from her desk drawer. "This is our consulting contract. While working on this project, you are not considered a Lethe employee and will not receive shares, benefits, or protections from Lethe. You will be paid commensurate to your skill level, and at the rate agreed. The contract terminates automatically after six weeks, unless both parties agree to extend the contract. Before, during, and after this project you are forbidden from disclosing the focus of the project with anyone other than your Lethe contact. Do you have any questions?"

Long looked over the paperwork. "Do you have the work of the previous groups that tried to decrypt this cube?"

"Would it be useful?" Sonya tilted her head.

"Knowing what they tried and what failed will save me time." And it would tell him who she had trusted.

Another small frown. "The other experts said they didn't want to be influenced by other people's processes." There was a hit of censure in her tone.

"We all approach work differently," he said. "I will probably look at it before reviewing their notes, but I don't feel the need to reinvent the wheel. Appearing like a genius to the world usually involves standing on the backs of geniuses who came before. It's how I did the decryption that I published in university."

Sonya gave a small nod, but he could see that she'd deducted a few points from the imaginary tally. "In that case, I'll make their work available to you. The records and a machine to process it on will arrive tomorrow. It goes without saying that everything stored on the computer becomes the property of Lethe after the contract is over."

"Of course." He made a mental note to scrub the machine for spyware and keep it away from his work lab and notes when it arrived. Lethe hadn't made their empire by playing fair.

Sonya stood up. "Then all is in order."

Following her lead, he stood too.

She posed, probably trying to look seductive. "I look forward to working with you, Doctor Long."

"And I look forward to working with you." As much as he looked forward to being eaten alive by ant lions. It was a trap, and the only way to escape was to move forward. If he could get Sonya the information maybe—just maybe—he'd escape with his life.

Keep reading! Head to
<u>www.inkprintpress.com/</u>
<u>lianabrooks/malik/change/</u>
to buy your copy now!

ABOUT THE AUTHOR

Liana is a fulltime writer, sometimes editor, and on-call kid wrangler who swears she has never stolen anything in her life. Well, okay, there was the lipstick at her friend's house when she was six, but she put it back the next day because she felt guilty.

Lockpicks? What lockpicks?

Oh! Those lockpicks sitting next to the writing desk? That's just research.

When she isn't being perfectly normal and average, Liana enjoys writing science fiction in every form, from sprawling space opera romances (the *Fleet of Malik* series) to the antics of a super-powered family (the *Heroes and Villains* series). Liana also writes the *All I Want For Christmas* novellas.

You can learn more about her and her books at www.LianaBrooks.com.

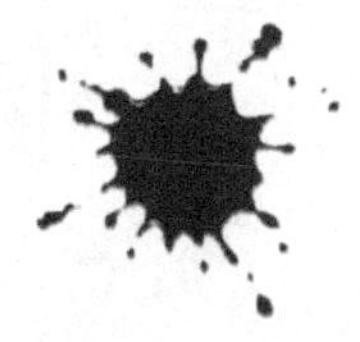

INKLETS

Collect them all! Released on the 1st and 15th of each month.

INKLET #055
Allure
AMY LAURENS

INKLET #056
The LIES We KNOW
LIANA BROOKS

DOUBLE ISSUE
INKLET #057
AFTERMATH & Fool Me Once
AMY LAURENS

INKLET #058
Purity
An Age Of Unicorns Story
AMY LAURENS

INKLET #059
Saved
AMY LAURENS

INKLET #060
A Kiss is the Secret
AMY LAURENS

INKLET #061
A Changing Tides Story
Fire Bright
AMY LAURENS

INKLET #062
Hades AND Persephone
LIANA BROOKS

INKLET #063
Just So Long As You're Happy
AMY LAURENS

INKLET #064
Theft Of A Lifetime
LIANA BROOKS

INKLET #065
Shoe
AMY LAURENS

INKLET #066
Published AUTHOR
LIANA BROOKS

DOUBLE ISSUE
INKLET #067
THE REMARKABLE INSIGHT OF JELLYBEANS & Understanding
AMY LAURENS

INKLET #068
Desperate Measures
AMY LAURENS

INKLET #069
Rock-a-bye
LIANA BROOKS

INKLET #070
the Other Carly
AMY LAURENS

INKLET #071
By By Bioluminescent Light
AMY LAURENS

INKLET #072
Even Villains Grant Wishes
A Heroes & Villains Story
LIANA BROOKS

www.ingramcontent.com/pod-product-compliance
Lightning Source LLC
Chambersburg PA
CBHW030810190726
48285CB00003B/1119